Preface to The Lyrical Ballads

William Wordsworth

The First Volume of these Poems has already been submitted to general perusal. It was published, as an experiment which, I hoped, might be of some use to ascertain, how far, by fitting to metrical arrangement a selection of the real language of men in a state of vivid sensation, that sort of pleasure and that quantity of pleasure may be imparted, which a Poet may rationally endeavour to impart.

I had formed no very inaccurate estimate of the probable effect of those Poems: I flattered myself that they who should be pleased with them would read them with more than common pleasure: and on the other hand I was well aware that by those who should dislike them they would be read with more than common dislike. The result has differed from my expectation in this only, that I have pleased a greater number, than I ventured to hope I should please.

For the sake of variety and from a consciousness of my own weakness I was induced to request the assistance of a Friend, who furnished me with the Poems of the ANCIENT MARINER, the FOSTER-MOTHER'S TALE, the NIGHTINGALE, the DUNGEON, and the Poem entitled LOVE. I should not, however, have requested this assistance, had I not believed that the poems of my Friend would in a great measure have the same tendency as my own, and that, though there would be found a difference, there would be found no discordance in the colours of our style; as our opinions on the subject of poetry do almost entirely coincide.

Several of my Friends are anxious for the success of these Poems from a belief, that if the views, with which they were composed, were indeed realized, a class of Poetry would be produced, well adapted to interest mankind permanently, and not unimportant in the multiplicity and in the quality of its moral relations: and on this account they have advised me to prefix a systematic defence of the theory, upon which the poems were written. But I was unwilling to undertake the task, because I knew that on this occasion the Reader would look coldly upon my arguments, since I might be suspected of having been principally influenced by the selfish and foolish hope of *reasoning* him into an approbation of these particular Poems: and I was still more unwilling to undertake the task, because adequately to display my opinions and fully to enforce my arguments would require a space wholly disproportionate to the nature of a preface. For to treat the subject with the clearness and coherence, of which I believe it susceptible, it would be necessary to give a full account of the present state of the public taste in this country, and to determine how far this taste is healthy or depraved; which again could not be determined, without pointing out, in what manner language and the human mind act and react on each other, and without retracing the revolutions not of literature alone but likewise of society itself. I have therefore altogether declined to enter regularly upon this defence; yet I am sensible, that there would be some impropriety in abruptly obtruding upon the Public, without a few words of introduction, Poems so materially different from those, upon which general approbation is at present bestowed.

It is supposed, that by the act of writing in verse an Author makes a formal engagement that he will gratify certain known habits of association, that he not only thus apprizes the Reader that certain classes of ideas and expressions will be found in his book, but that others will be carefully excluded. This exponent or symbol held forth by metrical language must in different aeras of literature have excited very different expectations: for example, in the age of Catullus Terence and Lucretius, and that of Statius or Claudian, and in our own country, in the age of Shakespeare and Beaumont and Fletcher, and that of Donne and Cowley, or Dryden, or Pope. I will not take upon me to determine the exact import of the promise which by the act of writing in verse an Author in the present day makes to his Reader; but I am certain it will appear to many persons that I have not fulfilled the terms of an engagement thus voluntarily contracted. I hope therefore the Reader will not censure me, if I attempt to state what I have proposed to myself to perform, and also, (as far as the limits of a preface will permit) to explain some of the chief reasons which have determined me in the choice of my purpose: that at least he may be spared any unpleasant feeling of disappointment, and that I myself may be protected from the most dishonorable accusation which can be brought against an Author, namely, that of an indolence which prevents him from endeavouring to ascertain what is his duty, or, when his duty is ascertained prevents him from performing it.

The principal object then which I proposed to myself in these Poems was to make the incidents of common life interesting by tracing in them, truly though not ostentatiously, the primary laws of our nature: chiefly as far as regards the manner in which we associate ideas in a state of excitement. Low and rustic life was generally chosen because in that situation the essential passions of the heart find a better soil in which they can attain their maturity, are less under restraint, and speak a plainer and more emphatic language; because in that situation our elementary feelings exist in a state of greater simplicity and consequently may be more accurately contemplated and more forcibly communicated; because the manners of rural life germinate from those elementary feelings; and from the necessary character of rural occupations are more easily comprehended; and are more durable; and lastly, because in that situation the passions of men are incorporated with the beautiful and permanent forms of nature. The language too of these men is adopted (purified indeed from what appear to be its real defects, from all lasting and rational causes of dislike or disgust) because such men hourly communicate with the best objects from which the best part of language is originally derived; and because, from their rank in society and the sameness and narrow circle of their intercourse, being less under the action of social vanity they convey their feelings and notions in simple and unelaborated expressions. Accordingly such a language arising out of repeated experience and regular feelings is a more permanent and a far more philosophical language than that which is frequently substituted for it by Poets, who think that they are conferring honour upon themselves and their art in proportion as they separate themselves from the sympathies of men, and indulge in arbitrary and capricious habits of expression in order to furnish food for fickle tastes and fickle appetites of their own creation.[1]

I cannot be insensible of the present outcry against the triviality and meanness both of thought and language, which some of my contemporaries have occasionally introduced into their metrical compositions; and I acknowledge that this defect where it exists, is more dishonorable to the Writer's own character than false refinement or arbitrary innovation, though I should contend at the same time that it is far less pernicious in the sum of its consequences. From such verses the Poems in these volumes will be found distinguished at least by one mark of difference, that each of them has a worthy *purpose* Not that I mean to say, that I always began to write with a distinct purpose formally conceived; but I believe that my habits of meditation have so formed my feelings, as that my descriptions of such objects as strongly excite those feelings, will be found to carry along with them a *purpose*. If in this opinion I am mistaken I can have little right to the name of a Poet. For all good poetry is the spontaneous overflow of powerful feelings; but though this be true, Poems to which any value can be attached, were never produced on any variety of subjects but by a man who being possessed of more than usual organic sensibility had also thought long and deeply. For our continued influxes of feeling are modified and directed by our thoughts, which are indeed the representatives of all our past feelings; and as by contemplating the relation of these general representatives to each other, we discover what is really important to men, so by the repetition and continuance of this act feelings connected with important subjects will be nourished, till at length, if we be originally possessed of much organic sensibility, such habits of mind will be produced that by obeying blindly and mechanically the impulses of those habits we shall describe objects and utter sentiments of such a nature and in such connection with each other, that the understanding of the being to whom we address ourselves, if he be in a healthful state of association, must necessarily be in some degree enlightened, his taste exalted, and his affections ameliorated.

I have said that each of these poems has a purpose. I have also informed my Reader what this purpose will be found principally to be: namely to illustrate the manner in which our feelings and ideas are associated in a state of excitement. But speaking in less general language, it is to follow the fluxes and refluxes of the mind when agitated by the great and simple affections of our nature. This object I have endeavoured in these short essays to attain by various means; by tracing the maternal passion through many of its more subtle windings, as in the poems of the IDIOT BOY and the MAD MOTHER; by accompanying the last struggles of a human being at the approach of death, cleaving in solitude to life and society, as in the Poem of the FORSAKEN INDIAN; by shewing, as in the Stanzas entitled WE ARE SEVEN, the perplexity and obscurity which in childhood attend our notion of death, or rather our utter inability to admit that notion; or by displaying the strength of fraternal, or to speak more philosophically, of moral attachment when early associated with the great and beautiful objects of nature, as in THE BROTHERS; or, as in the Incident of SIMON LEE, by placing my Reader in the way of receiving from ordinary moral sensations another and more salutary impression than we are accustomed to receive from them. It has also been part of my general purpose to attempt to sketch characters under the influence of less impassioned feelings, as in the OLD MAN TRAVELLING, THE TWO THIEVES, &c. characters of which the elements are simple, belonging rather to nature than to manners, such as exist now and will probably always exist, and which from their constitution may be distinctly and profitably contemplated. I will not abuse the indulgence of my Reader by dwelling longer upon this subject; but it is proper that I should mention one other circumstance which distinguishes these Poems from the popular Poetry of the day; it is this, that the feeling therein developed gives importance to the action and situation and not the action and situation to the feeling. My meaning will be rendered perfectly intelligible by referring my Reader to the Poems entitled POOR SUSAN and the CHILDLESS FATHER, particularly to the last Stanza of the latter Poem.

I will not suffer a sense of false modesty to prevent me from asserting, that I point my Reader's attention to this mark of distinction far less for the sake of these particular Poems than from the general importance of the subject. The subject is indeed important! For the human mind is capable of excitement without the application of gross and violent stimulants; and he must have a very faint perception of its beauty and dignity who does not know this, and who does not further know that one being is elevated above another in proportion as he possesses this capability. It has therefore appeared to me that to endeavour to produce or enlarge this capability is one of the best services in which, at any period, a Writer can be engaged; but this service, excellent at all times, is especially so at the present day. For a multitude of causes unknown to former times are now acting with a combined force to blunt the discriminating powers of the mind, and unfitting it for all voluntary exertion to reduce it to a state of almost savage torpor. The most effective of these causes are the great national events which are daily taking place, and the encreasing accumulation of men in cities, where the uniformity of their occupations produces a craving for extraordinary incident which the rapid communication of intelligence hourly gratifies. To this tendency of life and manners the literature and theatrical exhibitions of the country have conformed themselves. The invaluable works of our elder writers, I had almost said the works of Shakespeare and Milton, are driven into neglect by frantic novels, sickly and stupid German Tragedies, and deluges of idle and extravagant stories in verse.-- When I think upon this degrading thirst after outrageous stimulation I am almost ashamed to have spoken of the feeble effort with which I have endeavoured to counteract it; and reflecting upon the magnitude of the general evil, I should be oppressed with no dishonorable melancholy, had I not a deep impression of certain inherent and indestructible qualities of the human mind, and likewise of certain powers in the great and permanent objects that act upon it which are equally inherent and indestructible; and did I not further add to this impression a belief that the time is approaching when the evil will be systematically opposed by men of greater powers and with far more distinguished success.

Having dwelt thus long on the subjects and aim of these Poems, I shall request the Reader's permission to apprize him of a few circumstances relating to their *style*, in order, among other reasons, that I may not be censured for not having performed what I never attempted. Except in a very few instances the Reader will find no personifications of abstract ideas in these volumes, not that I mean to censure such personifications: they may be well fitted for certain sorts of composition, but in these Poems I propose to myself to imitate, and, as far as possible, to adopt the very language of men, and I do not find that such personifications make any regular or natural part of that language. I wish to keep my Reader in the company of flesh and blood, persuaded that by so doing I shall interest him. Not but that I believe that others who pursue a different track may interest him likewise: I do not interfere with their claim, I only wish to prefer a different claim of my own. There will also be found in these volumes little of what is usually called poetic diction; I have taken as much pains to avoid it as others ordinarily take to produce it; this I have done for the reason already alleged, to bring my language near to the language of men, and further, because the pleasure which I have proposed to myself to impart is of a kind very different from that which is supposed by many persons to be the proper object of poetry. I do not know how without being culpably particular I can give my Reader a more exact notion of the style in which I wished these poems to be written than by informing him that I have at all times endeavoured to look steadily at my subject, consequently I hope it will be found that there is in these Poems little falsehood of description, and that my ideas are expressed in language fitted to their respective importance. Something I must have gained by this practice, as it is friendly to one property of all good poetry, namely good sense; but it has necessarily cut me off from a large portion of phrases and figures of speech which from father to son have long been regarded as the common inheritance of Poets. I have also thought it expedient to restrict myself still further, having abstained from the use of many expressions, in themselves proper and beautiful, but which have been foolishly repeated by bad Poets till such feelings of disgust are connected with them as it is scarcely possible by any art of association to overpower.

If in a Poem there should be found a series of lines, or even a single line, in which the language, though naturally arranged and according to the strict laws of metre, does not differ from that of prose, there is a numerous class of critics who, when they stumble upon these prosaisms as they call them, imagine that they have made a notable discovery, and exult over the Poet as over a man ignorant of his own profession. Now these men would establish a canon of criticism which the Reader will conclude he must utterly reject if he wishes to be pleased with these volumes. And it would be a most easy task to prove to him that not only the language of a large portion of every good poem, even of the most elevated character, must necessarily, except with reference to the metre, in no respect differ from that of good prose, but likewise that some of the most interesting parts of the best poems will be found to be strictly the language of prose when prose is well written. The truth of this assertion might be demonstrated by innumerable passages from almost all the poetical writings, even of Milton himself. I have not space for much quotation; but, to illustrate the subject in a general manner, I will here adduce a short composition of Gray, who was at the head of those who by their reasonings have attempted to widen the space of separation betwixt Prose and Metrical composition, and was more than any other man curiously elaborate in the structure of his own poetic diction.

In vain to me the smiling mornings shine,
And reddening Phoebus lifts his golden fire:
The birds in vain their amorous descant join,
Or chearful fields resume their green attire:
These ears alas! for other notes repine;
A different object do these eyes require;
My lonely anguish melts no heart but mine;
And in my breast the imperfect joys expire;
Yet Morning smiles the busy race to cheer,
And new-born pleasure brings to happier men;
The fields to all their wonted tribute bear;
To warm their little loves the birds complain.
I fruitless mourn to him that cannot hear
And weep the more because I weep in vain.

  It will easily be perceived that the only part of this Sonnet which is of any value is the lines printed in Italics: it is equally obvious that except in the rhyme, and in the use of the single word "fruitless" for fruitlessly, which is so far a defect, the language of these lines does in no respect differ from that of prose.

Is there then, it will be asked, no essential difference between the language of prose and metrical composition? I answer that there neither is nor can be any essential difference. We are fond of tracing the resemblance between Poetry and Painting, and, accordingly, we call them Sisters: but where shall we find bonds of connection sufficiently strict to typify the affinity betwixt metrical and prose composition? They both speak by and to the same organs; the bodies in which both of them are clothed may be said to be of the same substance, their affections are kindred and almost identical, not necessarily differing even in degree; Poetry[2] sheds no tears "such as Angels weep," but natural and human tears; she can boast of no celestial Ichor that distinguishes her vital juices from those of prose; the same human blood circulates through the veins of them both.

If it be affirmed that rhyme and metrical arrangement of themselves constitute a distinction which overturns what I have been saying on the strict affinity of metrical language with that of prose, and paves the way for other distinctions which the mind voluntarily admits, I answer that the distinction of rhyme and metre is regular and uniform, and not, like that which is produced by what is usually called poetic diction, arbitrary and subject to infinite caprices upon which no calculation whatever can be made. In the one case the Reader is utterly at the mercy of the Poet respecting what imagery or diction he may choose to connect with the passion, whereas in the other the metre obeys certain laws, to which the Poet and Reader both willingly submit because they are certain, and because no interference is made by them with the passion but such as the concurring testimony of ages has shewn to heighten and improve the pleasure which co-exists with it. It will now be proper to answer an obvious question, namely, why, professing these opinions have I written in verse? To this in the first place I reply, because, however I may have restricted myself, there is still left open to me what confessedly constitutes the most valuable object of all writing whether in prose or verse, the great and universal passions of men, the most general and interesting of their occupations, and the entire world of nature, from which I am at liberty to supply myself with endless combinations of forms and imagery. Now, granting for a moment that whatever is interesting in these objects may be as vividly described in prose, why am I to be condemned if to such description I have endeavoured to superadd the charm which by the consent of all nations is acknowledged to exist in metrical language? To this it will be answered, that a very small part of the pleasure given by Poetry depends upon the metre, and that it is injudicious to write in metre unless it be accompanied with the other artificial distinctions of style with which metre is usually accompanied, and that by such deviation more will be lost from the shock which will be thereby given to the Reader's associations than will be counterbalanced by any pleasure which he can derive from the general power of numbers. In answer to those who thus contend for the necessity of accompanying metre with certain appropriate colours of style in order to the accomplishment of its appropriate end, and who also, in my opinion, greatly under-rate the power of metre in itself, it might perhaps be almost sufficient to observe that poems are extant, written upon more humble subjects, and in a more naked and simple style than what I have aimed at, which poems have continued to give pleasure from generation to generation. Now, if nakedness and simplicity be a defect, the fact here mentioned affords a strong presumption that poems somewhat less naked and simple are capable of affording pleasure at the present day; and all that I am now attempting is to justify myself for having written under the impression of this belief.

But I might point out various causes why, when the style is manly, and the subject of some importance, words metrically arranged will long continue to impart such a pleasure to mankind as he who is sensible of the extent of that pleasure will be desirous to impart. The end of Poetry is to produce excitement in coexistence with an overbalance of pleasure. Now, by the supposition, excitement is an unusual and irregular state of the mind; ideas and feelings do not in that state succeed each other in accustomed order. But if the words by which this excitement is produced are in themselves powerful, or the images and feelings have an undue proportion of pain connected with them, there is some danger that the excitement may be carried beyond its proper bounds. Now the co-presence of something regular, something to which the mind has been accustomed when in an unexcited or a less excited state, cannot but have great efficacy in tempering and restraining the passion by an intertexture of ordinary feeling. This may be illustrated by appealing to the Reader's own experience of the reluctance with which he comes to the re-perusal of the distressful parts of Clarissa Harlowe, or the Gamester. While Shakespeare's writings, in the most pathetic scenes, never act upon us as pathetic beyond the bounds of pleasure--an effect which is in a great degree to be ascribed to small, but continual and regular impulses of pleasurable surprise from the metrical arrangement.-- On the other hand (what it must be allowed will much more frequently happen) if the Poet's words should be incommensurate with the passion, and inadequate to raise the Reader to a height of desirable excitement, then, (unless the Poet's choice of his metre has been grossly injudicious) in the feelings of pleasure which the Reader has been accustomed to connect with metre in general, and in the feeling, whether chearful or melancholy, which he has been accustomed to connect with that particular movement of metre, there will be found something which will greatly contribute to impart passion to the words, and to effect the complex end which the Poet proposes to himself.

If I had undertaken a systematic defence of the theory upon which these poems are written, it would have been my duty to develope the various causes upon which the pleasure received from metrical language depends. Among the chief of these causes is to be reckoned a principle which must be well known to those who have made any of the Arts the object of accurate reflection; I mean the pleasure which the mind derives from the perception of similitude in dissimilitude. This principle is the great spring of the activity of our minds and their chief feeder. From this principle the direction of the sexual appetite, and all the passions connected with it take their origin: It is the life of our ordinary conversation; and upon the accuracy with which similitude in dissimilitude, and dissimilitude in similitude are perceived, depend our taste and our moral feelings. It would not have been a useless employment to have applied this principle to the consideration of metre, and to have shewn that metre is hence enabled to afford much pleasure, and to have pointed out in what manner that pleasure is produced. But my limits will not permit me to enter upon this subject, and I must content myself with a general summary.

I have said that Poetry is the spontaneous overflow of powerful feelings: it takes its origin from emotion recollected in tranquillity: the emotion is contemplated till by a species of reaction the tranquillity gradually disappears, and an emotion, similar to that which was before the subject of contemplation, is gradually produced, and does itself actually exist in the mind. In this mood successful composition generally begins, and in a mood similar to this it is carried on; but the emotion, of whatever kind and in whatever degree, from various causes is qualified by various pleasures, so that in describing any passions whatsoever, which are voluntarily described, the mind will upon the whole be in a state of enjoyment. Now if Nature be thus cautious in preserving in a state of enjoyment a being thus employed, the Poet ought to profit by the lesson thus held forth to him, and ought especially to take care, that whatever passions he communicates to his Reader, those passions, if his Reader's mind be sound and vigorous, should always be accompanied with an overbalance of pleasure. Now the music of harmonious metrical language, the sense of difficulty overcome, and the blind association of pleasure which has been previously received from works of rhyme or metre of the same or similar construction, all these imperceptibly make up a complex feeling of delight, which is of the most important use in tempering the painful feeling which will always be found intermingled with powerful descriptions of the deeper passions. This effect is always produced in pathetic and impassioned poetry; while in lighter compositions the ease and gracefulness with which the Poet manages his numbers are themselves confessedly a principal source of the gratification of the Reader. I might perhaps include all which it is *necessary* to say upon this subject by affirming what few persons will deny, that of two descriptions either of passions, manners, or characters, each of them equally well executed, the one in prose and the other in verse, the verse will be read a hundred times where the prose is read once. We see that Pope by the power of verse alone, has contrived to render the plainest common sense interesting, and even frequently to invest it with the appearance of passion. In consequence of these convictions I related in metre the Tale of GOODY BLAKE and HARRY GILL, which is one of the rudest of this collection. I wished to draw attention to the truth that the power of the human imagination is sufficient to produce such changes even in our physical nature as might almost appear miraculous. The truth is an important one; the fact (for it is a *fact*) is a valuable illustration of it. And I have the satisfaction of knowing that it has been communicated to many hundreds of people who would never have heard of it, had it not been narrated as a Ballad, and in a more impressive metre than is usual in Ballads.

Having thus adverted to a few of the reasons why I have written in verse, and why I have chosen subjects from common life, and endeavoured to bring my language near to the real language of men, if I have been too minute in pleading my own cause, I have at the same time been treating a subject of general interest; and it is for this reason that I request the Reader's permission to add a few words with reference solely to these particular poems, and to some defects which will probably be found in them. I am sensible that my associations must have sometimes been particular instead of general, and that, consequently, giving to things a false importance, sometimes from diseased impulses I may have written upon unworthy subject; but I am less apprehensive on this account, than that my language may frequently have suffered from those arbitrary connections of feelings and ideas with particular words, from which no man can altogether protect himself. Hence I have no doubt that in some instances feelings even of the ludicrous may be given to my Readers by expressions which appeared to me tender and pathetic. Such faulty expressions, were I convinced they were faulty at present, and that they must necessarily continue to be so, I would willingly take all reasonable pains to correct. But it is dangerous to make these alterations on the simple authority of a few individuals, or even of certain classes of men; for where the understanding of an Author is not convinced, or his feelings altered, this cannot be done without great injury to himself: for his own feelings are his stay and support, and if he sets them aside in one instance, he may be induced to repeat this act till his mind loses all confidence in itself and becomes utterly debilitated. To this it may be added, that the Reader ought never to forget that he is himself exposed to the same errors as the Poet, and perhaps in a much greater degree: for there can be no presumption in saying that it is not probable he will be so well acquainted with the various stages of meaning through which words have passed, or with the fickleness or stability of the relations of particular ideas to each other; and above all, since he is so much less interested in the subject, he may decide lightly and carelessly.

 Long as I have detained my Reader, I hope he will permit me to caution him against a mode of false criticism which has been applied to Poetry in which the language closely resembles that of life and nature. Such verses have been triumphed over in parodies of which Dr. Johnson's Stanza is a fair specimen.

> "I put my hat upon my head,
> And walk'd into the Strand,
> And there I met another man
> Whose hat was in his hand."

 Immediately under these lines I will place one of the most justly admired stanzas of the "*Babes* in the Wood."

> "These pretty Babes with hand in hand
> Went wandering up and down;
> But never more they saw the Man
> Approaching from the Town."

In both of these stanzas the words, and the order of the words, in no respect differ from the most unimpassioned conversation. There are words in both, for example, "the Strand," and "the Town," connected with none but the most familiar ideas; yet the one stanza we admit as admirable, and the other as a fair example of the superlatively contemptible. Whence arises this difference? Not from the metre, not from the language, not from the order of the words; but the *matter* expressed in Dr. Johnson's stanza is contemptible. The proper method of treating trivial and simple verses to which Dr. Johnson's stanza would be a fair parallelism is not to say this is a bad kind of poetry, or this is not poetry, but this wants sense; it is neither interesting in itself, nor can *lead* to any thing interesting; the images neither originate in that sane state of feeling which arises out of thought, nor can excite thought or feeling in the Reader. This is the only sensible manner of dealing with such verses: Why trouble yourself about the species till you have previously decided upon the genus? Why take pains to prove that an Ape is not a Newton when it is self-evident that he is not a man.

I have one request to make of my Reader, which is, that in judging these Poems he would decide by his own feelings genuinely, and not by reflection upon what will probably be the judgment of others. How common is it to hear a person say, "I myself do not object to this style of composition or this or that expression, but to such and such classes of people it will appear mean or ludicrous." This mode of criticism so destructive of all sound unadulterated judgment is almost universal: I have therefore to request that the Reader would abide independently by his own feelings, and that if he finds himself affected he would not suffer such conjectures to interfere with his pleasure.

If an Author by any single composition has impressed us with respect for his talents, it is useful to consider this as affording a presumption, that, on other occasions where we have been displeased, he nevertheless may not have written ill or absurdly; and, further, to give him so much credit for this one composition as may induce us to review what has displeased us with more care than we should otherwise have bestowed upon it. This is not only an act of justice, but in our decisions upon poetry especially, may conduce in a high degree to the improvement of our own taste: for an *accurate* taste in Poetry and in all the other arts, as Sir Joshua Reynolds has observed, is an *acquired* talent, which can only be produced by thought and a long continued intercourse with the best models of composition. This is mentioned not with so ridiculous a purpose as to prevent the most inexperienced Reader from judging for himself, (I have already said that I wish him to judge for himself;) but merely to temper the rashness of decision, and to suggest that if Poetry be a subject on which much time has not been bestowed, the judgment may be erroneous, and that in many cases it necessarily will be so.

I know that nothing would have so effectually contributed to further the end which I have in view as to have shewn of what kind the pleasure is, and how the pleasure is produced which is confessedly produced by metrical composition essentially different from what I have here endeavoured to recommend; for the Reader will say that he has been pleased by such composition and what can I do more for him? The power of any art is limited and he will suspect that if I propose to furnish him with new friends it is only upon condition of his abandoning his old friends. Besides, as I have said, the Reader is himself conscious of the pleasure which he has received from such composition, composition to which he has peculiarly attached the endearing name of Poetry; and all men feel an habitual gratitude, and something of an honorable bigotry for the objects which have long continued to please them: we not only wish to be pleased, but to be pleased in that particular way in which we have been accustomed to be pleased. There is a host of arguments in these feelings; and I should be the less able to combat them successfully, as I am willing to allow, that, in order entirely to enjoy the Poetry which I am recommending, it would be necessary to give up much of what is ordinarily enjoyed. But would my limits have permitted me to point out how this pleasure is produced, I might have removed many obstacles, and assisted my Reader in perceiving that the powers of language are not so limited as he may suppose; and that it is possible that poetry may give other enjoyments, of a purer, more lasting, and more exquisite nature. But this part of my subject I have been obliged altogether to omit: as it has been less my present aim to prove that the interest excited by some other kinds of poetry is less vivid, and less worthy of the nobler powers of the mind, than to offer reasons for presuming, that, if the object which I have proposed to myself were adequately attained, a species of poetry would be produced, which is genuine poetry; in its nature well adapted to interest mankind permanently, and likewise important in the multiplicity and quality of its moral relations. From what has been said, and from a perusal of the Poems, the Reader will be able clearly to perceive the object which I have proposed to myself: he will determine how far I have attained this object; and, what is a much more important question, whether it be worth attaining; and upon the decision of these two questions will rest my claim to the approbation of the public.

Original footnotes

^ It is worth while here to observe that the affecting parts of Chaucer are almost always expressed in language pure and universally intelligible even to this day.

^ I here use the word "Poetry" (though against my own judgment) as opposed to the word Prose, and synonomous with metrical composition. But much confusion has been introduced into criticism by this contradistinction of Poetry and Prose, instead of the more philosophical one of Poetry and Science. The only strict antithesis to Prose is Metre.

THE END

Printed in Great Britain
by Amazon